THE GETTYSBURG LETTER

PATRICK E. CRAIG

"Cover by Cora Graphics Cora Bignardi—www.coragraphics.it

This is a work of fiction. Names, characters, places, and incidents are products of the authors' imaginations or are used fictitiously. Any resemblance to actual persons, living or dead, is entirely coincidental.

Copyright © 2019 by Patrick E. Craig

P&J Publishing P.O. Box 73, Huston, Idaho 83630

Library of Congress Cataloging—The Gettysburg Letter / Patrick E. Craig

ISBN 978-1-7347635-3-9 (pbk.)

ISBN 978-1-7347635-4-6 (eBook)

All rights reserved. No part of this publication may be reproduced, stored in a retrieval system, or transmitted in any form or by any means—electronic, mechanical, digital, photocopy, recording, or any other—except for brief quotations in printed reviews, without the prior permission of the publisher.

Printed in the United States of America

To all the dreamers

CONTENTS

A Note From Patrick E. Craig   vii

Part I
THE LETTER — 1863

The Diary of Ginnie Wade	3
1. The March - June 12, 1863	7
2. West Fort — June 13, 1863	11
3. Winchester — June 14, 1863	15
4. Old Friends — June 15, 1863	17
The Diary of Ginnie Wade	21
5. When Johnny Comes Marching — June 30, 1863	25
6. The Coming Storm — June 30, 1863	29
The Diary of Ginnie Wade	31
7. On The Move — July 1, 1863	33
8. Skirmish — July 1, 1863	35
The Diary of Ginnie Wade	39
9. Culp's Hill — July 2, 1863	41
10. The Old Tree — July 2, 1863	45
The Diary of Ginnie Wade	51

Part II
THE LETTER - 2013

11. Homecoming — July 2, 2013	55
The Diary of Ginnie Wade	59
12. Ginnie — July 2, 2013	63
13. Awakening — July 2, 1863	67
14. The Last Battle — July 3	71
The Diary of Ginnie Wade	75
15. The Letter — July 3 – 10:00 A.M	77
16. Going Back — July 3 – 12:00 P.M	83
17. Back to Gettysburg — July 4, 2013	87

18. Special Delivery — July 5   91

Epilogue   97

About the Author   101
Also by Patrick E. Craig   103

A NOTE FROM PATRICK E. CRAIG

Vignette: *a brief incident or scene as in a play or a book...*

This is a short, romanticized version of the story of Ginnie Wade, John Wesley Culp, and Jack Skelly, a vignette as it were. Though they are historical figures and there are many facts and also many legends surrounding their lives, the thread of this story sprang from my own imagination. What we do know is that at the battle of Winchester, Jack Skelly, a wounded Union Soldier, wrote a letter to his betrothed, Ginnie Wade, who lived in Gettysburg. He gave the letter to their childhood friend, Wesley Culp, who was fighting for the South, and asked him to deliver it to Ginnie. The contents of the letter and what happened to it are subject to much speculation and so I have joined in. My part in that speculation created an imaginary diary written by Ginnie Wade that I have used to tie this story together. As far as I know, the diary never existed except on these pages. It is my hope that my theories concerning this event will, as you read The Gettysburg Letter, be at least entertaining and hopefully thought-provoking. Enjoy!

Patrick E. Craig

I

THE LETTER — 1863

THE DIARY OF GINNIE WADE

June 15 - 1863

I have spent this day with the terrible feeling I will never see Jack again. It has haunted all my waking hours. The commonplace doings of life in Gettysburg have faded into the fabric of this fear that clutches at my heart. Our boys are in Virginia somewhere fighting Robert E. Lee. I have, up to this point, not feared for Jack, as I know him to be a good and capable soldier dedicated to the Union cause. But this morning, when I awoke, there was a certainty that something terrible has happened or is about to happen to my beloved, and I cannot free myself from it. I pray that this dread is my imagination, and not some divine instillation from above. Oh, Jack, may the sheltering hand of Providence be with you.

GINNIE SIGHED AND PUT DOWN THE PEN. She reached for a handkerchief lying by her hand and dabbed her eyes. The fabric smelled of lavender, her mother's lavender. Jack loved the smell of lavender and she had worn it that day they pledged their love. It was a day of splendor and beauty, his hand gently touching hers, his powerful arms lifting her to the top of a rock overlooking Cunningham Falls. The fall sun filtered through the golden leaves of the trees and pale rays of light crowned them. He stood with her, looking into her eyes. She remembered her heart pounding, an unfamiliar heat rushing to her face.

When had she started loving Johnston Kelly? They had always been friends, but there came a day when suddenly she was shy when he came into the room. He had been a friend, Ginnie and Jack. They laughed and played together with all the others—David, Wesley, Willie. Up on Culp's hill, around the farmhouse, by their tree. One day they were kids, and the next, he was a man...

"Oh, Jack!"

She could not push away the dread that filled her heart. She did not know where this feeling came from. She had been so sure that Jack would come home to her. He was two weeks late, but he had promised...

"Ginnie! Ginnie, stop your lollygaggin'! I need you to go to your sister's house. She's going to have that baby any minute."

Ginnie crashed back to reality. "Yes, Mama." She stood up and went to the window. The town of Gettysburg spread before her. The heat of summer had burned away the morning mist, and the town lay still, as if waiting.

Waiting for the Rebs.

The Rebs were coming, as sure as the day was hot, they were coming. Riders had come from the South. Lee had crossed the Potomac. They had pushed Hooker's army to the Northeast, and now they were coming to Gettysburg.

And somewhere between Lee and Ginnie was the 87th Pennsylvania, and in that troop of brave Union boys was Jack Skelly.

His lips had burned hers like fire that day on the mountain, and she had answered him back with a passion that made her shy to think of. Jack, her only always love.

Dear God, Bring him home to me.

1

THE MARCH - JUNE 12, 1863

The sun was a caldron in an otherwise empty sky. The blazing heat beat down on the dusty road. The soldiers in gray were slowly moving into columns. It was the middle of June and Richard Ewell's Second Corps was headed toward Winchester. All of the top commanders—Rodes, Ewell, Early, Johnson, and the old man himself, Robert E. Lee – had met together the night before and now the Army of Northern Virginia was on the move again.

Wesley Culp stuffed the last of his things into his pack, tied it up, and left the field where his Company was bivouacked. All around him the Rebel Army was moving onto the road that led north up the Shenandoah Valley. They had been moving north for days and they were tired, but the men of this Army didn't care. They had been beating the pants off the Federals for months and they were in high spirits. Now the rumors were flying. Wesley's tent-mate, Jed Culpepper smiled as he fell into step beside Wes.

"We're headed to Pennsylvania for sure, Wes. Lee is going to take this war to old Abe and we're going to end it once and for all."

Wesley, felt a sharp pang of regret at the words. Pennsylvania was his home state and most of his family was fighting for the North. Jed kept on.

"Ain't yer brother fighting for the Yanks?"

"When the war broke out, my brother, William and my cousin, David, joined Company F, 87th Pennsylvania. My best friend, Jack Skelly, joined up with them."

"How come you didn't go back to Pennsylvania and fight with them?" Jed asked.

"When I moved to Virginia, I was only fifteen. I made new friends and when they all joined the local militia, the Hamtramck Guards, I joined too. At first it was just a social club, but when the war started, we all joined up. I thought the fight would be over in a couple of weeks, but I was wrong."

Jed looked over at Wes. "The word is that the 87th is up at Winchester."

Wesley shook his head. "Well, Jed, I shore don't want to run up agin' Willie and David or Jack Skelly in Winchester. It would be a shame to have to shoot at 'em."

"Well, if you do see 'em in battle, you'll shoot, won't you Wes?"

" I reckon I'll have to, Jed."

Wesley got a look on his face that said he didn't want to talk about it anymore, so Jed shut up. The two men marched along in silence. All around them the grey army moved inexorably like a flood—pouring out of the South in what they hoped would be the campaign that would force the Federals to take their hands off and leave them alone.

The 2nd Virginia had just come from some of the worst fighting of the war at Chancellorsville where they had crushed Hooker's army and pushed it north. Now the Southern troops were invading the North, forcing the Army of the Potomac to leave Washington D.C. and confront them. Everyone knew that a big fight was coming and the Army of Northern Virginia was ready.

Jed pulled a chunk of chaw out of his pocket, offered some to

Wes, and when Wes shook his head no, bit off a big piece. In a few minutes he looked like a cow chewing its cud. He spit and then started talking again.

"I hear that Billy Yank has re-built those forts up there at Winchester. Old Milroy's gonna have his Bluebellies hunkered down up on them hills just waiting for us with some artillery."

Wesley grinned.

"What are you worried for, Jed? You sound like an old woman. Those Yanks will break and run just like they always do. Besides, we got to get in there and rescue those folks from that butcher."

Wesley reached in his pocket and pulled out a folded up piece of paper.

"Listen to this. The Yanks were passing these out and some of our boys got a hold of them."

He read out loud.

In this city (Winchester) of about 6,000 inhabitants ... my will is absolute law—have none dare contradict or dispute my slightest word or wish. The secesh here have heard many terrible stories about me before I came and supposed me to be a perfect Nero for cruelty and blood, and many of them both male and female tremble when they come into my presence to ask for small privileges, but the favors I grant them are slight and few for I confess I feel a strong disposition to play the tyrant among these traitors.
— Robert H. Milroy

"I tell you, Jed, we got to go up there and drive that devil out."
Jed looked at his friend.
"Well, I reckon that's what we'll do, then, Wes."
The two marched on in silence.

2

WEST FORT — JUNE 13, 1863

The 2nd Virginia marched all night. Around five o'clock in the morning, dark gray clouds began to move in from the West – a thunderhead stirred up by the oppressive heat. In the distance the marching column could hear deep rumbles breaking the stillness of the just-dawning day. Jed held his hand out palm up, looking for drops of rain.

"Looks like we're in fer some rain today, Wes"

"That ain't rain, you greenhorn, that's cannon. Sounds like Milroy's got his batteries going up at West Fort, firin' at some of our skirmishers, no doubt. Early's moving toward town, over in the West."

"How come Ewell split us up? How come we don't just all go in at once, straight at 'em?" Jed asked.

A bearded sergeant marching next to the two men guffawed.

"Don't you know nothin' 'bout tactics? We're coming in on the east side so the Bluebellies will think we're the main attack. Meanwhile, Early's taking his boys right into town on the Valley Pike. I heard the Captain say that Rodes was swinging around behind the Federals through Martinsburg to cut off any escape.

We're going to wrap these Yankees up and send 'em home in a box."

He turned to the troops behind him and yelled out, "C'mon boys, we're gonna take care of ol' Milroy and then it's straight on to Washington DC We'll have Honest Abe wearin' gray by the fourth of July."

A ragged cheer lifted from the throats of the men around Wesley. The spirit of the Army of Northern Virginia was high.

"I sure wish Stonewall Jackson was here to see this," said a buckskinned private behind Wes. "He'd be proud of us, that's for sure."

Around eight-thirty in the morning, while moving northwest on the Front Royal Pike, the 2nd Virginia came up to the Opequon River crossing. There were a few Federal pickets stationed there, but the rebel skirmishers quickly drove them off. Some Union cavalry made an attempt to harass the line at Hoge Run an hour later but they were also driven off. Finally just before noon, Johnson's division came within range of the guns at Fort Garibaldi.

Wes and Jed watched while officers rode up and down the line yelling for the boys to find cover. Most of the men got off the road and into the ditches and behind trees. Wes and Jed lay behind a picket fence while shells screamed overhead

"We're pretty much sittin' ducks out here, Wes."

"Yep! And it looks like we'll be stuck here until Early gets into town."

The bearded sergeant, who was sitting close by, laughed again and pointed up to the heights above them.

"Men, I don't believe Milroy has any idea that he's facin' the entire Second Corps of Lee's Army. He's got all his men concentrated up there in them three forts. If he had any brains he would have fallen back to Harper's Ferry. He must be pretty confident. But we're going to sweep them out of those forts in the morning, so get fed and get some rest."

That night the storm that had been threatening the army all day arose and a strong rain drenched Winchester and the lower valley all night long. Wes and Jed sat under a tarp watching the rain pour down.

"Do you think Willie's up in one of them forts?" Jed asked.

"I don't know, Jed. After this is over, I'm sure I'm going to see some Pennsylvania boys. I hope Willie, David and Jack aren't with them."

3

WINCHESTER — JUNE 14, 1863

The rain died down early in the morning and with the dawn came more skirmishing. Wes and the rest of the boys were moved to the right to extend their lines around the east side of the Union forces. They ran into a few patrols outside Winchester but fighting was light. Word came down the line that Gordon's brigade had captured Bower's Hill and placed batteries there and Early's brigade was marching to another position north of town. Around ten o'clock in the morning the orders came. A captain rode up on a lathered horse and got the men up. He called all the officers together. Wes could see him pointing to the right. In a few minutes, Sergeant Williams came back. He pointed to Wes and Jed and a number of other men.

"I want you boys to eat now, but eat quick because you're gonna be at it all day. We have to keep their attention until Early gets in position this afternoon."

The 2nd Virginia advanced a line of skirmishers on the right to occupy the Federals' attention, providing diversionary skirmishing all day from 10 a.m. until about 4 p.m. Around six, Wes and his companions were startled by a huge roar of artillery coming from the north side of town. Wes grabbed Jed by the arm as a cheer went up from the troops.

"That's Early, he's got his cannon going. It won't be long now."

At eight o'clock another rider came down the road from the north. He was shouting and waving his hat.

"Early's got them on the run. He's taken West Fort and the Yankees are all holed up in Fort Garabaldi. They can't take the pounding that Early's artillery is giving them and they'll probably try to get out sometime during the night. You boys have to cut them off."

The officers got the men to form ranks and they set off on the double-quick. The sky grew dark but the men kept moving. Jed kept up a stream of chatter as he marched along with Wes.

"Where we headed, Wes? You know this place?"

"This is the Berryville Pike. If Milroy runs he's going to move up the Martinsburg Pike, and then cut over onto the Old Charles Town Road. We'll catch up with him at Stephenson's Depot."

4

OLD FRIENDS — JUNE 15, 1863

It was near dawn. The sky was just turning purple over the hills to the East. The men of the 2nd Virginia were moving quietly toward the intersection of the Valley Pike and old Charles Town Road. Word came down the line to halt. After a quiet conference with the Colonel, the Captain gathered his men around.

"Our scouts have seen the Federals. The head of Milroy's column is just ahead comin' into the crossroads. We're headed up to the railroad bridge with some artillery. The rest of the regiment will deploy along Milburn Road. We'll catch them between us as they come up to the bridge."

The men moved into position. Wes and Jed crouched alongside the others in the shadow of the bridge. Wes peered ahead. The morning was finally coming and he could see down the road to the south. Someone shouted.

"There they are!"

Wesley and his friends laid their muskets over the edge of the road and waited for the command. It came soon enough.

"Fire!"

A sheet of flame erupted from the massed muskets. Wesley

watched the front row of Yankees go down like wheat in a wind. Screams of the wounded drifted back up to them as they quickly reloaded. More Confederates moved up and joined them. The men in blue were massing for an attack.

"They're coming again!"

Again came the sheet of flame and again an invisible hand sheared the blue coats down. Men from Nichol's regiment were steadily reinforcing the 2nd Virginia. To the side and rear, Wes could hear rebel cannon pounding down on the Yankee column. There was one more attack and then Wes could see the flags of the Stonewall Brigade moving up behind the Yankees. What was left of Milroy's force threw down their guns and scattered in every direction. A great cheer went up from the rebel lines as the white flag was hoisted.

Wesley looked over at Jed. Jed had a long cut across the side of his head where a musket ball had grazed him and his face was bloody, but it couldn't hide the grin.

"We done it, Wes. They're quitting."

WESLEY CULP MOVED among the prisoners that were gathered along the road. He was looking for men from the 87th Pennsylvania.

"Any of you boys seen the 87th?" he asked as he went.

A young private looked up. He had been shot through the cheek and his face was a mask of blood. He opened his mouth but half his teeth were gone and he couldn't speak, so he lifted his hand and pointed. Wesley followed the outstretched hand. A short distance away he could see a group of men. On their shoulders they wore the insignia of the 87th Pennsylvania. There! Among them, his old friend, Johnny Parkwood!

"Johnny!"

Johnny looked up. A shock of recognition crossed his face.

"Wes?"

The two men embraced and then stepped apart. The men around Johnny gave them a queer look. Johnny pointed to Wes.

"This is my boyhood chum, Wesley."

"What's he doin' in that there uniform?" a grizzled sergeant with a bloody cloth tied around his head snarled.

"I've lived in the South since I was fifteen and now, it's my home. I couldn't fight against my neighbors," Wesley said. "Johnny can we speak?"

The two men stepped aside and spoke quietly.

"Where's Willie and David, Johnny?"

"I don't know, Wes. When your boys came up behind us, the new men threw down their guns and took off runnin'. After that the whole line broke. A bunch of the men got away. I hope they are headed back home. Wes, I got bad news."

"What, Johnny?"

"It's about Jack Skelly...he's shot pretty bad."

"Where is he?"

Johnny led Wesley to a row of wounded who were stretched out by the side of the road. Among them Wes saw his friend, Jack Skelly. His sleeve was torn open and the surgeons were working on his arm. Wesley knelt down beside him and touched Jack on the shoulder. Jack's eyes opened.

"Wes? Is that you?"

"Yes, Jack, I'm here. How goes it?"

"Passin' good, Wes, passin' good."

They both chuckled at the old soldier's private joke.

"How is he, Doctor?" Wes asked.

The surgeon shook his head.

"He's lost a lot of blood and his arm is tore up pretty bad. He'll probably lose it."

Jack stirred and tried to lift up on his good arm, but the pain was too much and he fell back.

"I don't think I'll be going home, Wes, nor Johnny neither. You fellas seem to be headed north and you'll probably be in Pennsylvania in a few days. You must do something for me."

"What, Jack? I'll do whatever you want."

Jack Skelly fumbled in his breast pocket and pulled out an envelope. There was a smear of blood on it. Wes could see the name written there.

Ginnie Wade.

"Wes, if you're in Gettysburg, you've got to get this letter to Ginnie. She was expecting me home two weeks ago. Please, Wes."

Wes took the letter.

"I'll make sure she gets it, Jack."

Jack took hold of Wesley's arm and pulled himself up. He stared into Wes's face with burning eyes.

"Swear, Wes! Swear you'll get that letter to Ginnie!"

"On my life, Jack. I swear on my life. I'll get this letter to Ginnie somehow."

THE DIARY OF GINNIE WADE

June 22, 1863

Rumors abound! The people of Gettysburg are in a commotion, for it is a certainty that Robert E. Lee and the Army of Northern Virginia are marching into Pennsylvania. Sally Meyers was over and she says that some of our boys from the 87th just got home. They were in a battle in Winchester, Virginia, last Sunday. Willie Culp and David Myers were among those that have returned. Willie told Sally the Rebs killed or captured a Captain, two Lieutenants and a lot of good Pennsylvania men. I am waiting to hear from Willie or David as to the whereabouts of Jack. I cannot shake this terrible feeling that he is among the captured or even worse. What will I do? I do not know if life would be worth living without Jack...

GINNIE STOOD ON HER PORCH. Willie Culp and David Meyers stood beside her, watching more Union boys straggle into town. The word was out: Lee beat the northern troops soundly at

Winchester and Brandy Station and now Jeb Stuart's cavalry had gotten across and were riding wildly through the countryside to the north of their town. The survivors of the fights in Virginia were now arriving in Gettysburg in droves.

David put his hand on Ginnie's arm. "Gosh, Ginnie, if I knew where Jack was, I would tell you. They caught up to us on the old Charles Town Road. There was a lot of them, more than we could handle."

Willie nodded. "It was the whole damned Army of Northern Virginia. When they fired on us, a lot of the green boys turned and ran. There wasn't enough of us left to fight it out. So we lit out, too."

Ginnie blushed. "Willie, your language."

"Sorry, Ginnie, but that's what they are. If we'd a had more men, we would have whupped 'em sure. Lee was just too much for us. He gave Old Joe Hooker a real lickin' at Chancellorsville, but at least we killed Stonewall Jackson. That old devil won't be walkin' on Union ground, that's for sure, and I hope he roasts in hell."

Ginnie blushed again and turned to David. "When did you last see Jack, David?"

"I don't remember seeing him in the battle, but I saw him the night before at mess."

"Did he say anything about me, David?"

David shook his head. "He said he was writing you a letter, but he hadn't finished it yet. We didn't talk much—we was all tired and hungry and then our sergeant rousted us out for picket duty, and I didn't see him again."

Willie piped up. "I seen him at the battle, Ginnie. When the Rebs broke our line, he stayed with some of the boys to give us cover. I didn't see him after that cause we was scattered everywhere. I seen some of the boys who stayed behind later, so I'm pretty sure he musta got out too."

"How did he look, Willie? Was he all right?"

Willie grinned. "Aww, Ginnie. Jack Skelly was always the toughest of all of us. If anyone will get through this war, Jack will."

David "He'll be fine, Ginnie. He'll be fine. Why I expect you'll see him come marching up the road any time now."

More troops in blue clogged the road. Ginnie looked at each passing face, hoping against hope. But in that sea of faces, she did not see Jack.

5

WHEN JOHNNY COMES MARCHING — JUNE 30, 1863

The weather since Winchester had been unseasonable, rain at night, showers during the day. Wesley and the men of Ewell's Corps marched north. They were headed up the Shenandoah Valley behind the sheltering mask of the Blue Mountains. Wesley's thoughts were gloomy. He remembered the look on Jack's face as the stretcher bearers carried him away. Wesley knew where they were headed—first a hospital and then, if Jack lived, Libby prison in Richmond. It was the closest prisoner of war camp. That hell-hole was only surpassed by Andersonville for suffering and starvation, and Wesley was torn inside as he watched Jack put up on a wagon with the other wounded Union prisoners. His old friend waved weakly with his good arm, and tried to smile, but his face was pale and drawn and his shoulders slumped in defeat.

What is this about—brother against brother, neighbor against neighbor? Jack's going to a horrible prison in the South and I'm marching north to fight against my family and my old friends. God, what are you up to? There is no rhyme or reason to this...

On June 15, two days after their victory at Winchester, Wesley and the boys of the 2nd Virginia crossed the Potomac at Williamsport with the rest of the Army of Northern Virginia and began the invasion of the North. Once they were in Maryland, Ewell divided his corps. He sent Early through Gettysburg to Wrightsville, while Rodes and Johnson went north. A.P. Hill and Longstreet were coming along behind. Almost 70,000 rebels were marching through the heart of Union territory. Pennsylvania was swarming with gray clad troops.

Wes and his companions were marching, marching, marching—until it seemed that their feet were disconnected from the rest of their body—just moving on their own. Even Jed stopped his incessant chatter and trudged along quietly, head down, as though measuring each step.

Wes reached into his jacket pocket and touched the leather pouch that held the letter. He had to get to Gettysburg somehow—he had sworn an oath to Jack. But they were skirting to the west, hidden behind the mountains to avoid the eyes of the Federals. After the decisive victory at Winchester, morale was high, but Wes was burdened by his promise to Jack Skelly.

"Jed, I'm never going to get this letter to Ginnie. We're going to take Harrisburg and then we'll move east and south, to go chase ol' Abe out of Washington."

Wes spit and shifted his musket to his left shoulder. Jed tried to be conciliatory.

"I don't know, Wes. You may get back to Gettysburg. You've been pretty lucky so far. Hopefully you'll stay alive long enough."

Jed cackled at his own prophecy, but Wes was not amused.

"Yeah, well you're the one who got shot at Winchester. Too bad they didn't aim lower. How was they to know that your blamed head is harder than a cannonball? That mine´ ball just ricocheted off. Probably killed three of our boys in passin'."

The rain began in earnest. It was early in the day but the clouds and rain made it seem late. Wes shifted his musket again.

His shoulders ached, he was soaked to the skin and his stomach was empty. Wes noticed that they were passing a lot more barns and houses.

"We must be comin' into Harrisburg, Jed. I used to travel up here with David to the State Fair, bringing produce from my Uncle Henry's farm."

Wes paused, thinking of happier days—him and Willie and David...and Jack Skelly – riding through the Pennsylvania countryside on the way to market, or hunting together up at Tumbling Run.

"To hell with this war!"

Just then a rider went tearing by, heading toward the front of the column. After a few minutes the command came down the line to halt. The men stood at ease, wondering what this latest development meant. Soon the company commanders were called up to where General Ewell and his staff were.

"Hey, Sarge!" one of the men called out. "Can we start a fire and dry out? I'm soaked to the bone."

"Hold your horses, men! Let's find out what all the fuss is about first."

In about half an hour, the word came down to reverse their direction. Their Colonel gathered his officers around and explained what was happening. Wes and Jed stood close enough to hear.

"Men, a large contingent of Federal troops has been spotted moving toward Gettysburg. General Lee has ordered that the whole army turn and converge there. Looks like we're in for a big fight. Early is coming back from Wrightsville and we'll meet him outside of Carlisle. A.P. Hill and Longstreet are bringing their men in from Chambersburg down the Cashtown Road. Heth is out front and he outta be in Gettysburg this afternoon. We have to move up quick and reinforce him. We don't have time to stop, so if you have any of that hardtack we liberated at Winchester, eat it now."

There was no grumbling. This was what the men had been waiting for—a chance to meet the Yankees on their home ground. There was a momentary confusion as the ranks reformed to move south, and then the whole division began to move inexorably through the Pennsylvania countryside. Wesley touched the letter in his pocket again.

"Glory be, Jed. I'm gonna get to see Ginnie after all."

6

THE COMING STORM — JUNE 30, 1863

Gray storm clouds swept in from the west. The 2nd Virginia moved down the Carlisle Road toward Gettysburg. About fifteen miles out of town they halted. More couriers had come in and the orders passed down the line. Sergeant Williams pulled his platoon leaders aside.

"Now listen up and listen good. General Lee has sent orders that we are not to engage until the whole army has moved up to Gettysburg. Our patrols reported Union soldiers threw a line across the road outside of town. We don't know how many or who they are, so we're sitting tight for the night. A.P. Hill has gone into camp on the far side of town, waitin' for Longstreet. I imagine we'll move into Gettysburg sometime tomorrow."

"How come we don't know who's in front of us, Sergeant?" a Corporal asked. "I thought Stuart was supposed to let us know where the Federals are."

Sergeant Williams took a suck on his cold pipe.

"Well, it seems that our lovely Gineral Stuart has been joyriding up north, gittin' hisself in the papers as he loves to do, but not doin' this here army any good. I bet the Old Man is hoppin' mad. So now we're going in blind. There could be some scouts in front of us or Reynolds' whole Corps. Nobody knows. That's why we're staying here tonight. Hopefully they'll get it sorted out tomorrow."

Later that night Wes and Jed sat by the fire, sipping some coffee and trying to get dry. Jed knocked out his pipe and filled it with fresh tobacco. He lifted the pipe in a salute to nobody in particular.

"Compliments of the great state of Pennsylvania. Best tabaccy I've had in many a day."

He took a few long puffs and sighed in satisfaction. He glanced over at Wes, who was sitting silently in front of the fire, watching the flames dance.

"How you gonna git the letter to yer friend's girl, Wes?"

Wes looked up.

"I'll tell the Sergeant I need to see my sister, Julia. He'll let me go because he's sweet on her. He fell for her when she used to visit me over at Shepardstown. He'll want me to put in a good word. Ginnie lives a few houses away on Breckenridge Street. I'll slip over and give her the letter and that will be that."

"Sounds like a plan, Wes. Well, we better turn in. Gonna be a brawl tomorrow and that's for sure."

THE DIARY OF GINNIE WADE

June 30, 1863

Today Union cavalry rode into Gettysburg. A handsome man with a mustache was leading them. There must have been an entire division, for they rode through town for a long time. Now we are sure that a great battle is coming for the soldiers rode out to the seminary, dismounted and took up positions on both sides of the Cashtown Road. We could see them in the cupola of the seminary tower, looking south. Late in the afternoon, a large group of soldiers rode back through town and headed up the Carlisle Road. They seem to be waiting, as we are, for Robert E. Lee and his army. I am worried for Georgia and her new baby.

"That's John Buford," Willie said, as he pointed to the tall soldier at the head of the horsemen. "He's a thumper, he is. He won't take any guff from Lee."

Ginnie stood quietly. There had been no word from Jack, and

her feeling of dread had slowly increased. Even the birth of her little nephew two days before had not cheered her up. The cavalrymen nodded and waved and tipped their hats to the pretty brunette on the porch, but Ginnie ignored them. She turned away and went inside the house.

7

ON THE MOVE — JULY 1, 1863

*A*t dawn the 2nd Virginia awakened to distant artillery fire to the south. The men scrambled out of their blankets and started packing. The Sergeant came around.

"Don't be so hasty, boys. Git some breakfast. That's probably just a few of our boys tradin' rounds with the Yanks. We'll be moving out soon enough."

Around eight o'clock, Wes and Jed were sitting with the men enjoying some fine Pennsylvania bacon when a rider came in. He headed straight toward the officers' tent. The Colonel, James Allen, rose and came out to meet him. The courier didn't bother to get down but started talking excitedly and pointing back down the Carlisle Road toward Gettysburg. After they finished, the Colonel strode back to where his officers were seated and spoke to them briefly. Immediately the men wolfed down the remains of their breakfasts and headed off.

"Looks like we'll be leavin' soon, Wes. Something's got the Colonel pretty excited."

Their captain came over and gathered his lieutenants and sergeants around.

"Boys, it seems that Harry Heth has stumbled into a brawl

outside of town with a bunch of dismounted cavalry—probably John Buford's men. They're a tough bunch—held against us at Thorofare Gap for six hours. They've thrown a line across the Cashtown Road and now A.P. Hill and his Corps are bottled up behind Heth in the gap that passes through the hills. We need to get down into town and flank them on the left, take the pressure off Heth. We have a fifteen-mile march. Now move!"

The troops scrambled to break down their tents and half-shelters. Wes felt an excitement grow. He always felt it before he went into battle. In a few minutes the officers started riding by, shouting the command to move out. They were on their way to Gettysburg.

8

SKIRMISH — JULY 1, 1863

Wesley Culp stood on Middle Street in Gettysburg and looked up the hill. Just a short distance away, at the very end of the street, stood his Uncle Henry's farmhouse. Jed leaned on his musket a few feet away. They were both near exhaustion. They had come down the Carlisle Road late in the afternoon and instead of Buford's Cavalry they had run straight into Oliver Howard's XI Corps to the north of town.

When they figured out who they were facing, Sergeant Williams pointed over at the Union lines.

"Boys, we've met these Germans before. We fought them at Chancellorsville and we made 'em run. Oliver Howard was in command. It's the same troops and the same commander. We broke 'em then and we'll break 'em now."

Colonel Allen rode up and gathered his officers. He pointed to the Union line on the left.

"Right there, boys, I want you to hit them right there. That's where they're weak. Hit and hit hard. They'll roll up like a rug."

Sure enough, when the Virginians went after them, the Union troops broke and ran, just like Chancellorsville. The Rebels followed them through town and watched as the Yankees scrambled up the backside of Culp's Hill. Wesley's regiment was itching to follow, but Ewell and Early had ridden up and stopped the attack. Now with darkness coming on Wes and Jed were watching with amazement as their officers debated on a course of action. General Ewell, General Early and several officers were standing and looking up at Culp's Hill. An old man in a General's uniform was standing in front of Ewell, shouting at him.

"Who is that, Wes?" Jed asked.

"That's General Isaac Trimble," Wes replied. "He's a firebrand."

They listened while Trimble berated Ewell. The old man was waving his arms and pointing.

"General, we have got to take that hill. There is no one up there yet."

General Ewell stood looking at Trimble. He said nothing. Trimble was furious.

"General Jackson would not have stopped like this. Not with the Bluebellies on the run, no guns set up, and plenty of light left."

Still Ewell said nothing.

"Sir, I beg you," shouted Trimble. "Give me one division and I will take that hill."

Ewell stared at Trimble, but remained silent.

"Give me one brigade and I will take that hill."

Ewell blinked and put his arms behind his back.

"Sir, give me one regiment and I will take that hill."

General Ewell said nothing but simply shook his head. Trimble snatched his sword out of its scabbard and threw it at Ewell's feet.

"You, sir, are a disgrace, and this decision will come back to haunt you. Reynolds and Hancock will move in there tonight and fortify that blessed bloody hill and tomorrow there will be hell to pay! I assure you that General Lee will hear about this from me, personally."

The old man turned and walked away, while Wes and Jed stared after him. Colonel Allen's mouth was open in amazement. Ewell stared after Trimble and then shook his head again. General Early whispered something in Ewell's ear and Ewell nodded his assent. He gave the order for the troops to stand down.

Jed put his pack down and sat down beside the road. "Well, Wes. Looks like we ain't going up there tonight."

Wesley Culp smiled and patted the letter in his pocket. "That's just fine with me, Jed. Now I can go see Ginnie."

THE DIARY OF GINNIE WADE

July 1, 1863

This morning at dawn gunfire awakened us. The battle had started! The constant roar of the cannon and the muskets was terrifying. Two hours later, more Federal troops arrived in town. They came up the Baltimore Pike and headed through town toward the Cashtown Road. Around ten o'clock, Mother and I left our house and went to McClellan House to stay with Georgia until the baby comes. We could hear the battle going on for a while, and then the Rebel troops started pushing our boys back. Soon there was a flood of blue uniforms pouring by the house. Mother and I baked bread this morning and have been passing it out to our soldiers and filling their canteens from the well as they retreat through town. They are going up on Cemetery Ridge. The men we talk to say that A. P. Hill is right behind them. I wish Jack were here. He would know what to do. But I don't think he's ever coming.

Ginnie knew that something terrible had happened to Jack, she could feel it in her whole being. He was captured, or wounded, or maybe even...

I can't think about that! I must keep my faith. Jack told me he would come back to me.

She looked down at the garment she had been trying to repair and saw she had veered off a bit. She pulled the stitches out and started over. A quiet knock on the back door startled her. Ginnie got up, went to the door and opened it. David was standing there. He held his finger to his lips and whispered.

"The Rebs are coming into town. Buford held them, kept them jammed up in the Cashtown Gap until General Reynolds could get his infantry up to help. Buford's twenty-five hundred cavalrymen held off twenty-thousand Rebs. If they hadn't Lee's army would have come straight through town and they'd be up on Cemetery Hill now and we'd have the devil to pay. Stay inside. I don't think the Rebs will bother you, but just be safe."

Ginnie nodded, and then the tears came.

"What, Ginnie?"

"Jack's never coming back, I just know it. And... and..."

"What is it, Ginnie?"

"He never got to tell me he loved me, before he left. I was supposed to see him once more, but they were ordered out before dawn and he was gone before I got up."

David shook his head. "Jack loves you, Ginnie. I know he does."

Ginnie stared at David.

But a girl needs to hear it, David.

There was a sound outside and David moved to the door. "I gotta go Ginnie. I got to get up with my men."

Ginnie hugged David. "Be careful, David."

He grinned. "I will, Ginnie, and I know you will hear from Jack, I just know it."

9

CULP'S HILL — JULY 2, 1863

Wesley Culp awakened as the night began to turn. He slipped on his boots and pulled his jacket around him. Faint morning light was pushing through a lowering sky that was still overcast with clouds, but a warm breeze was blowing up from the south, heralding a warm July day.

Good day for a fight.

He put his cap on, pulled back the tent flap, and looked out. No one was up yet except for the sentries. He checked in his pocket to make sure the letter was there and then started off toward his sister's house. The lookout stopped him on his way out of camp.

"Where ya headed, Wes?"

"Sergeant Williams gave me permission to visit my sisters. I want to make sure they're all right."

"You got family here?"

Wesley pointed at the red farmhouse just a few hundred feet away.

"That's my Uncle Henry's place. I used to play up on that hill there, Culp's Hill, when I was a kid. Me and my brother, Willie, and my cousin, David, and my sisters knew every inch of it."

Wesley pointed over to the right.

"That hill there is Raffensberger Hill. My Uncle Henry is married to Anna Raffensberger. Her parents own that place up there where the Yanks are dug in."

"How come you're fighting with us, if your family all lives here? Don't it bother you?"

Wesley pulled his coat tighter against the morning chill.

"Listen, I moved to Virginia almost ten years ago. My home is there now, and that's where most of my friends are. If you must know, it does feel strange to be back here, fighting against my family, but I'm in it now and there ain't nothin' I can do about it."

"Well, make sure you get back here soon. The Colonel said we're in for a big fight today."

Wesley headed up Middle Street into town. In just a few minutes he came to the home of Anna and Julia. He slipped around to the side door and knocked quietly. He heard someone coming and then the door opened a crack and Julia peeked out.

"Wes! What are you doing here?"

Julia reached out and grabbed Wesley and pulled him into the house. She glanced outside and then shut the door and turned to him.

"You need to be careful. The Union pickets are not far away."

Julia brushed some dust off his jacket and then pulled him into a hug. They held each other for a minute and then Julia stepped back and called out.

"Anna, come see."

Wes heard footsteps coming from the other room and then his sister, Anna, appeared in the kitchen doorway.

"Wesley! Thank the Lord!"

She rushed over and enveloped Wes in another hug. The three stood looking at each other. Then Julia spoke.

"Willie's home, David too."

Wesley's heart jumped. He pushed his hat back on his head.

"So they made it back. Well, Johnny Parkwood wasn't so lucky. He was taken prisoner and he's bound for Libby prison."

"Oh, Wes, that's terrible," Anna said.

Wesley looked around as if expecting to see his brother.

"When did Willie get back, and where is he?"

Julia went to the table and sat down.

"He just got home. He's up on the hill with David and the rest of the Union boys. He said they were in a battle at Winchester. Did you fight against them, Wesley?"

"Yes, I did. I had too. If you'd seen what that Milroy was doing to honest Virginian civilians, you'd have fought, too."

Anna pulled a handkerchief out of her apron and dabbed her eyes. Julia went on.

"Willie said they ran out of ammunition and retreated. The rest of their regiment was captured or killed so they just made for home. About a dozen of them came back. They were on the road for four days, poor boys. And Willie says…"

She paused and looked at Anna.

Anna broke in.

"Willie says you're a traitor and he doesn't ever want to speak to you or see you again."

Wesley pulled up a chair, sat down and looked down at the floor. He spoke quietly.

"Girls, I don't know why all this is happening this way. All I know is that I made my choice and I've got to stay with it. I'm sorry Willie feels that way. By the way I…I saw Jack Skelly after the battle."

Anna glanced at Julia.

"Oh, Ginnie will be so glad to hear. Where is he?"

"I don't think he'll be coming home. He was bad shot, and headed for one of our hospitals. He gave me a letter to give to her. I promised I'd see she got it. That's where I'm headed."

Julia put her hand to her mouth.

"Wesley, you can't go to see her."

"Why not? She only lives over on Breckenridge."

Julia grabbed Wesley's arm.

"She's not at her house, Wesley. She's over at Georgia's house."

"Her sister?"

"Yes. Georgia is having' a baby any time now, and Ginnie went over to Baltimore Street to help. The Rebs came in and now they are in between the lines. You can't get in there. The union troops are right behind Georgia's house."

"But I promised Jack. I swore an oath."

"Wesley, you're just going to have to wait until the battle's over."

10

THE OLD TREE — JULY 2, 1863

The men of the 2nd Virginia were stationed at the bottom of the east flank of Culp's Hill, waiting for something to happen. Away towards Little Round Top some artillery had begun to fire and the sound was growing in intensity. But Wesley was lost in thought and not paying too much attention. His attention was focused on the hill.

Right over there is where Willie broke his leg when he fell off that rock. And up there is the place where we dug out a fort in the ground and defended it against injuns.

Wesley looked further up the hill. There was the tree, towering over the rest of the hill. They had gathered there after chores on weekends and in the summer. It had been a special place for Wes.

Whenever I had a problem to work through, or somethin' to think about I went up to the tree. You can almost see Harrisburg from up there. And now Willie's up there somewhere with a gun, and probably some of the other good Pennsylvania boys, waiting to shoot me as soon as I show my head.

Just then Sergeant Williams came up. He beckoned to Wesley.

"Culp, come over here."

Wes jumped up and went over to the sergeant.

"Word's come down that Longstreet is attacking on the Union left flank, down by Little Round Top. Ewell is going to start a demonstration up here to keep Meade from reinforcing down at that end of the line. You know this hill. I want you to go up there as close as you can to the breastworks the Yanks have dug and keep an eye on any troops movin' in or out. If you see anything, come on back and tell me. Take Jed with you."

Wesley grabbed Jed and together they began to climb the rocky slope. Wesley led, keeping behind trees and boulders. It reminded him of the days when they used to take turns being the Injun and sneaking up on the fort. When they came to the tree, Wes motioned for Jed to stop. The tree was on a slight rise and they could see right over to the Union lines, only about two hundred feet away. Wesley could see blue hats moving behind the fortifications. Wes and Jed stayed low, just watching. There was some Rebel artillery fire going over from the direction of Benner's Hill to the Northeast and the Yanks were staying down. After a while, Wes heard someone on the other side shouting something. He watched as troops began to file out of the trenches and move off down the hill. They watched as the remaining Yankees moved out along the line to fill in the gaps. Wes put a finger to his lips and signaled for Jed to move back down the hill.

The sergeant saw them coming down. When they arrived at the bottom they were breathing hard from the climb.

"What's goin' on, Culp?"

"The Yankees have moved a bunch of men out. They're probably going down to help against Longstreet. The line up there is pretty thin. I bet we could sweep them if we attacked now."

The sergeant sent a runner down to the colonel but it was a long time until orders came back to get ready. By then it was getting late in the day. The troops assembled and waited. It wasn't until seven o'clock that the order came to attack the hill in strength. Wesley looked over at Jed.

"You be careful up there, Jed. Even though they're stretched thin, those defenses looked pretty strong."

"You too, Wes. Keep your head down."

Wesley patted his pocket. He had placed the letter inside a leather pouch for safe-keeping. He wondered if he would ever see Ginnie Wade.

The men of the 2nd Virginia began to move up the hill. Over to their left the men from Steuart and Williams' brigades were wading across Rock Creek and headed up beside them. Wesley pointed the way up the hill. It was hard going.

Whang!

A bullet ricocheted off a rock in front of Wesley. The Yanks had seen them comin'. More shots came and then a volley from the top of the hill. The Virginians pressed forward. They returned fire. A man to his left fell, his face a bloody mask. Wes could see the blue hats along the top of the wall ahead.

Trimble was right. We should of come up here before they built that wall. Now it's just like Fredricksburg only we're on the wrong side.

All around them the guns were firing continuously. The men in gray lifted up the strange and terrifying scream, the Rebel Yell, and rushed forward. Much smoke drifting—roar of battle—screams of men. The charge broke against the wall and the Rebels moved back. Piles of dead and dying men lay among the rocks. An officer came up behind them waving his sword.

"Forward men, don't retreat, move forward!"

The men turned and started back up the hill. More fire. The officer with the sword went down. The Virginians began to back down the hill to cover. Darkness fell on Culp's Hill. The firing died down. Wes and Jed crouched behind the tree, waiting for orders. Off to the left, the fighting picked up.

"That's Steuart's boys, Jed. Sounds like they're going at it."

A sergeant approached through the dark woods.

"C'mon you fellas, our boys have taken some of the trenches

over on the left. We need to push up there and dig those Yankees out. C'mon"

Once more the tired men of the 2nd Virginia gathered and began to move up the hill. The dark was a cloak of protection, but it also hid the enemy and they were almost on the Union defenses before they knew where they were. A rifle flash came from somewhere in front, and then a volley. All around them men were going down. The roar of the guns was deafening. Suddenly an explosive shell burst right above them. The force of the blast knocked Wesley and Jed flat. Wes lay there stunned, his ears ringing, the sound of the battle coming from a long way off. Slowly he came back to consciousness. Jed was lying motionless a few feet away. Wes crawled over to him and shook his shoulder.

"Jed! Jed! Are you okay?"

Shells continued to burst around them and Wes could hear the sound of musket balls cutting through the leaves of the tree above him. Jed groaned.

"Jed, are you hit?"

Jed moved beneath his hand and opened his eyes.

"What was that? I didn't even hear it coming."

"It was an explosive shell, Jed. It blew right above us."

"Whoa...are your ears ringing? I can barely hear you."

Wesley helped Jed sit up. Jed felt himself all over.

"Doesn't look like I'm wounded, Wes – just knocked flat."

Jed grinned.

"Well, you better get up. We're still in the middle of it."

The two men crawled behind the tree. There was a constant buzzing, whispering, zipping sound all around the tree. Behind them they heard a man's voice, urging them to get up and move forward. Wes pointed up the hill.

"C'mon, Jed, the Yankees are up there!

Men rose up out of the dark on both sides of them and started to advance toward the rock wall up the hill. Then another withering burst of fire poured down on them from up the hill. There was a strangled yell behind them and the voice that was urging them forward was suddenly cut off. The attack faltered and died as men went down all around them. They were crouched behind the tree when their captain came past. He looked at the two men and pointed down the hill.

"Culp, we're pulling out. You men get down off the hill. We'll come again tomorrow."

Wes looked at Jed.

"You heard what the Captain said. Now let's go!"

Wes got to his feet and moved out and Jed followed him back down the hill.

THE DIARY OF GINNIE WADE

July 2 - 1863

The Union soldiers have retreated from town and Gettysburg is filled with Rebels. Last night we could hear the Federal troops digging trenches and chopping trees up on the ridge. Mother says they will make a defense there. Just to the left of our house at the bottom of Cemetery Hill is a Union picket line and across the street the houses are filled with Confederate sharpshooters and so we are trapped at Georgia's house. Mother and I sneak out the back to give bread and water to our boys, but the situation is growing more dangerous. We will continue, because Jack would want me to help our men. My heart has grown heavy today thinking of my beloved. Willie Culp last saw Jack when the Pennsylvania troops were cut off as they tried to escape. Jack stayed behind to give cover to the boys who were retreating. That is so much like Jack. David said Jack wrote me a letter before the battle, so now I am waiting to hear from him. Every day I am drawn to the window to look for the post, but it is foolish for I know the letter will not come until this battle is over. Mother says the letter will never come, but I know that somehow Jack will find a way to reach me, if it takes a hundred and fifty years...

II

THE LETTER - 2013

HOMECOMING — JULY 2, 2013

Randy Culpepper drove the white 1996 Ford Explorer into the little town of Gettysburg, Pennsylvania. The SUV was covered with road dust that nearly obscured the California license plates. The temperature was in the mid-eighties and the ancient air-conditioning labored to keep up. The occasional showers only added to the humidity and it was like a sauna outside. The streets and roads all around Gettysburg were packed with cars and the village itself was jammed with people.

This was not the first time Randy had been to Gettysburg. He had come with his grandfather several times when he was younger, before the old man passed and Randy left for San Francisco. But this trip was special. It was the 150th anniversary of the Battle of Gettysburg. There was going to be a big celebration, lots of exhibits and re-enactments of the major battles. Randy was a Civil War buff. It was his grandfather's fault. There had been a special room at his grandfather's house in Richmond, Virginia, dedicated to his great-great grandfather, Jed Culpepper. Randy loved that room. All of Jed's civil war equipment was on display. The 1853 Enfield rifled musket hung on the wall beneath the stars and bars flag of the Confederacy. On a stand below the flag was

Jed's Colt 1851 Navy Revolver. When he was a kid, Randy often walked over to Grandpa's house after school. As he came up the street he could see the old man sitting on the front porch, reading the paper and smoking a cigar.

"Here for a history lesson, son?" Grandpa would ask.

"Yes, Sir!"

Then the two of them went in the house, walked down the hall and entered 'the room.' Randy would drop down on the floor—his grandfather sat in the old rocker by the window. The hours flew by as his grandfather told him the stories—the glorious first days of the war when the South could not be beaten and General Lee never left a battlefield in the hands of the enemy, the victories at Fredericksburg and Chancellorsville, First and Second Winchester and finally, the battle at Gettysburg.

Gettysburg! His grandfather didn't like the subject of Gettysburg. It was a sore point for sure.

"It was the turning point of the war, and even though Lee was like a god in the Southern states, it became obvious in later years that the 'Old Man' made major tactical blunders in his handling of the battle. Longstreet didn't want to fight there," Grandpa would say as he tapped his cigar ash into the flowerpot on the floor next to him.

"On the first day of the battle, Buford, the Union cavalry General, put a defensive line across the Cashtown Pike and kept A.P. Hill and Longstreet out of Gettysburg just long enough for John Reynolds to pack that bloody ridge with two Union corps. When Longstreet saw that the Federals held the good ground on Cemetery Hill, he advised Lee to slide south and east and pick another battlefield—ground of their choosing—in between Meade and Washington, D.C., where Meade would have to leave Gettysburg and attack them from a weaker position to protect the Capital."

"But Lee wouldn't listen, would he Grandpa?" Randy interjected. He knew the story by heart.

"No, son, he wouldn't listen. Lee was wrong and Longstreet was right. After the battle Lee admitted it to Ol' Pete, but by then it was too late. Lee never was able to mount another serious threat to the North and the next two years were spent mostly just escaping from the Federal troops."

"And Grandpa Jed was hurt there, right Grandpa?"

"Yep. My grandfather came home from Gettysburg without two of his fingers. He got them shot off when he was going for help for his best friend, Wesley Culp, after Wesley was badly wounded up on Culp's Hill. Grandpa lost his fingers and his best friend in that terrible battle."

They went together to visit the battlefield at least three times when Randy was in his teens. Grandpa took him to every spot on the battlefield and the names lived in Randy's heart: Seminary Ridge, The Wheat Field, The Peach Orchard, Little Round Top and Joshua Chamberlain's bayonet charge, Culp's Hill, and most glorious and heart-breaking of all – Pickett's Charge. Now, thirty years later, Randy was back in Gettysburg! This little town had hung like a millstone around the necks of all the citizens of the South since Lee's defeat. When it occurred to Randy that the Civil War Sesquicentennial was coming, he knew he had to come.

Grandpa will turn over in his grave if I'm not there...

So Randy closed down his landscaping business in Encino for two weeks, packed his gear, left his dog with his girlfriend and headed east. In the back of the SUV were the simple gray uniform of the 2nd Virginia Infantry, the Enfield and the Colt revolver that had belonged to Grandpa Jed, and the pack and half-tent that Jed had carried through many of the most famous battles. As he drove into town Randy saw hundred of campers and RVs parked along the road. Thousands of men in uniform were converging on Gettysburg from the North and the South, just as they had 150 years before. The two armies would meet again.

And I'll be there, Grandpa!

THE DIARY OF GINNIE WADE

July 2 - 1863

Around six o'clock this morning a bullet crashed through the window of Georgia's room, struck the bedpost and came to rest on the pillow where Georgia lay sleeping with her baby. If anybody is to die in this house today, I hope it is I, as Georgia has the baby to care for.

GEORGIA'S LABOR HAD BEEN LONG AND DIFFICULT. All during the first two days of the battle she had struggled, crying out in agony while explosions and gunfire wracked the village. It had taken the doctor a long time to get there and Ginnie had tried as best she could to make her sister comfortable.

"Ginnie, I swear I am about to burst. I am in as much pain as a human being can endure. Can't you do something?"

Ginnie had picked up a damp rag and swabbed Georgia's brow. "Don't fret, Georgie. The Doctor will come soon. He has to make his way through the back streets, and I'm sure he has other people to care for."

Finally the Doctor had come and from then on the delivery

went more smoothly. He had arrived in a rush, knocking with one hand and opening the door with the other. His face was wet from the heat and the sweat ran down his beard. "Good day ladies, Miss Ginnie. A fine day is it not? A fine day for a baby..." He glanced out the window. "Or a battle."

Ginnie had helped as best she could, what with Georgia yelling and the Doctor chatting away as though he were at a social.

"One more good one Miz McClellan then we'll have it." Then suddenly came a cry. And there he was.

That had been yesterday and now Ginnie stood looking down at her sleeping sister and her sweet new nephew. She held the spent bullet in her hand. It had come from somewhere down McKenzie Street. Georgia had been so tired that she hadn't even awakened, but the baby had been startled and it had taken Ginnie awhile to calm him.

She had held him close, smelling his fresh baby smell and feeling the softness of his hair. She had dreamed of having children with Jack, what it would be like raising a family here in Gettysburg, but the war had changed everything.

Why do things turn out the way they do? Here I'm dreaming of children and I don't even know if Jack wanted... wants to marry me.

Ginnie pulled the baby close.

I wish this were my baby. I wish that Jack was home and we were living on his Papa's place, with children, and a farm to run, and...

"Ginnie?" Her mother's voice broke the dream like a musket ball, like the one lying on the dresser.

"Yes, Mama?"

"We are out of bread for the soldiers. You must make some more. The flour is in the kitchen."

"Yes, Mama." Ginnie stood and laid the baby next to her sleeping sister. She stroked his face once more. Then she turned and went down the stairs.

She went to the bay window and looked out on the street,

hoping against hope. But Reb soldiers were everywhere. A tear ran down her cheek.

The postman won't come while the battle is raging. But he will come eventually and I will wait for Jack's letter. I will wait forever if I must.

12

GINNIE — JULY 2, 2013

Randy sat in the makeshift classroom while the commander of the 2nd Virginia delivered battle plans for the next day's rehearsal, complete with a Power Point presentation and laser pointer. The men were all wearing their uniforms. Muskets and packs leaned against the back wall.

"Those of you who have been here before know we won't be using the actual battlegrounds. Most of the battles will be at the Redding Farm, just north of town. You all need to be out there tomorrow for rehearsal. We will be setting up the encampments and the displays, and we need all the help we can get."

"What about the Blue-Gray Alliance show?" a bearded man in the back asked.

"They're done tonight. We won't actually be starting until the 4th of July, so we have time to get organized. See you all tomorrow."

Randy left the room with the rest of the men and headed back into town, carrying his pack and his Enfield. His hand felt the familiar dent on the stock as he walked. He'd been lucky to find a parking spot on Baltimore Street so he wasn't too far from the meeting. Above him the sky was clouding over.

Looks like we may get a thundershower tonight.

A few drops of rain began to fall and the smell of ozone rose from the heated asphalt. Up ahead he could see a sign—

Jennie Wade House, Museum, Ghostly Images.

Randy remembered the story. Jennie Wade had been the only civilian killed in the battle. She had died making bread for the Union soldiers who had a picket line behind her house.

There was something about a letter...

There was a flicker of lightning in the distance followed by a low rumble. As the flash of light pierced the darkness around the house he thought he saw a woman dressed in period costume standing at the top of the steps that led up from the street. Randy paused and looked up. It was hard to see her in the darkness but it looked like she was shaking her head as she stared up at the sign.

"Good evening, Ma'am. Can I help you with anything?"

"They got it all wrong."

"Wrong?"

"Yes. It's not supposed to read Jennie Wade. It's Ginnie Wade. Mary Virginia Wade. They got the sign all wrong. How will they know where to bring it?"

"Bring what, ma'am?"

"Why the letter, of course. Jack's letter."

"Jack's letter?"

An odd, cold sensation ran up Randy's back.

"Yes, Jack, my... my fiancée." She turned her head away for a moment and then lifted her shoulders and turned back. "At least I think he was my fiancée. He never really asked me to marry him before he went to Virginia to fight. There was a big battle down there and our boys got whipped pretty good. I never heard from him after that. Willie Culp came home and said that Jack had written me a letter before the battle. I think he was going to ask me. I'm sure Jack loved me..." She reached up and wiped away a tear. "I've been waiting and waiting..."

GINNIE — JULY 2, 2013

She's good! She's way into her part!

Randy looked closer at the woman. She was young and very pretty. Her hair was done up in a bun. Just then the sky lit up with a flash of lightning that was much closer. The bolt zigzagged across the sky followed by an enormous thunderclap right above them. Rain started—a few drops at first and then the sky opened and the rain poured down. Randy looked up at the sky and then turned back to the woman.

"You better get out of the rain..."

She was staring at him and now there was a strange glowing light all around her! Suddenly Randy was very cold...

Another bolt of lightning split the sky! It flashed right down on Randy and everything was lit up with a brilliant light. And enormous thunderclap sounded right over his head. Then a crushing blow slammed him down flat on his back and everything faded to nothing...

AWAKENING — JULY 2, 1863

A voice came from a long way off...
"Jed! Jed! Are you okay?"
There was a deafening, continuous roaring going on in the background and Randy could just make out the voice through it. Then he became aware of a strange whispering sound. He knew what it was—it was the sound of bullets cutting through the leaves of the tree above him.

Those are bullets!

"Jed, are you hit?"

There was a hand on his shoulder, shaking him and Randy opened his eyes.

"I didn't even see it coming."

"It was an explosive shell, Jed. It blew up right above us."

"No, I mean the lightning bolt...the one that hit me."

The man bending over him shook his head and grinned.

"That one was too close for comfort. But it wasn't lightning it was a shell. Now get up, Jed. We have to get to cover."

The man helped Randy sit up. Randy felt himself all over.

"Looks like I'm all in one piece—just knocked flat."

It was dark all around them. They were on a hillside. Further up the hill there was a continuous flashing of light along what looked like a breastwork made of logs and stones. It was musket fire…

Musket fire! Where the heck am I?

The man pulled on his arm.

"Well, you better get up. We're still in the middle of it."

Randy looked around in amazement.

"What is going on here?" he asked the man who was pulling on his arm.

"Just shut up and get behind the tree! And keep your fool head down!"

The man half-dragged half-shoved Randy behind the big tree. More explosive shells came down near them with a screaming roar and blew huge furrows in the ground. Randy could smell smoke and hear the screams of other men out in the dark.

Holy smoke! Those are live artillery shells!

He buried his face in the dirt. There was a constant buzzing, whispering, zipping sound all around the tree. Randy knew what it was. He had been under fire in Afghanistan and knew that terrible sound well. The men up behind that wall were shooting real bullets! Behind him he heard a man's voice, urging them to get up and move forward. The man who had helped him looked at Randy, and pointed up the hill.

"C'mon, Jed, the Yankees are up there!"

Randy looked at the man. He couldn't believe this was happening. Men rose up out of the dark on both sides of them and started to advance toward the rock wall up the hill. Then another withering burst of fire poured down on them from up the hill. There was a strangled yell behind them and the voice that was urging them forward was suddenly cut off. The attack faltered and died as men went down all around them. A man in a Confederate captain's uniform dove for cover behind the tree. He looked at the two men.

"Culp, we're pulling out. You men get down off the hill. We'll come again tomorrow."

Randy was frozen—he couldn't move. The man grabbed him and jerked him to his feet.

"If you want to die, stay here, Jed. You'll get killed for sure! Now let's go!"

Randy got to his feet and followed the man back down the hill. The terrain was rocky and several times Randy slipped and fell in the dark. Each time the man with him pulled him up.

"Tarnation, Jed, that shell must have knocked you stupid. You can't even walk."

When they got down off the hill they crossed a creek and came through the trees to a red barn. It looked like the soldiers had converted it into a hospital and men were lying inside and all around the building. There was a tent where men with blood-spattered aprons worked feverishly to help the wounded. Randy stared at the horrible scene with a sick feeling in his stomach.

This can't be happening!

The man with Randy leaned on his rifle with a sad expression on his face.

"I never thought I would see something like this on this farm."

Randy turned to the man.

"Look, you've got to help me understand. What in the world is happening here? Who are you and what am I doing here? And what is happening up on that hill? That's live ammunition being fired up there!"

The man smiled.

"Of course it's live ammunition. You think the Yankees are gonna blow us kisses?"

The man could see the confused look on Randy's face.

"Still haven't gotten over that blast, eh? Okay, let me help you. I am Wesley Culp, you are Jed Culpepper and we are smack in the middle of the biggest battle of this here war. And it just happens to be taking place on my Uncle John's farm."

Randy rubbed his forehead as he stared at Wesley.

"Wait a minute, now. That's not right. I'm not Jed Culpepper. I'm Randy Culpepper. Jed Culpepper was my great-great grandfather. The battle you are talking about happened one hundred and fifty years ago and Wesley Culp was killed there. He was Jed Culpepper's best friend. I came here to be in a re-enactment of that battle, but no one told me they were using live ammo. Now, why don't you tell me what's really happening? I just want to get out of here. This is crazy!"

Wesley looked at him with a patronizing smile and put an arm on Randy's shoulder.

"Jed, I think you better get some sleep. That shell knocked you silly. And if you don't think this is real, then what are those doctors doing with those men? And what about the boys who died up on that hill?"

"But you can't be Wesley Culp. I tell you Wesley Culp died one hundred and fifty years ago."

A flash of anger passed over Wesley's face and he reached out suddenly and slapped Randy.

"Pull yourself together, Jed Culpepper. You're talking crazy. Now you listen to me. I don't know what you're talking about and I don't care. All I care about is living through this fight. Now let's go get some rest, and I hope when you wake up you won't be talking all this nonsense."

Randy felt bile rising in his throat. He wanted to scream or hit something.

"Wesley, or whoever you are, I'm telling you that I do not belong here. And when I wake up I'm going to find out that this was all a dream."

"Whatever you say, Jed. Now let's go get some sleep."

He pointed at a red house among the trees.

"We can sleep in my Uncle John's cellar. I'm pretty sure our boys ran everyone out of there so Uncle John will never know. Come on."

14

THE LAST BATTLE — JULY 3

*R*andy Culpepper groaned and rolled over. He blinked his eyes and looked around. A small bit of light was coming through a vent in the wall above him. He was stretched out on a dirt floor wrapped in a thin blanket. A few feet away a man was sleeping on the ground. Randy heard the sound of artillery fire outside and then he remembered. He was in the cellar of Henry Culp's farmhouse at the bottom of Culp's Hill in the middle of the Battle of Gettysburg. The man sleeping next to him was John Wesley Culp. But that couldn't be, because John Wesley Culp died in 1863 and this was 2013. Or was it? A nearby shell blast shook the building and Randy sat straight up and yelled at the top of his voice.

"What is going on? This can't be happening!"

The man next to him stirred and woke up. He sat up and looked over at Randy.

"Are you still carrying on? I'm telling you, Jed, this is not the time to be acting like this. If I was you I'd just shut my mouth and do my duty."

The man began pulling on his boots.

"The boys in this outfit are all scared and some of them are looking for a way out of this battle. But acting crazy is a fool's game and it's not like you to shirk your duty. Nobody's gonna' believe you anyway, so you just might as well stop."

Randy stared at the man named Wes.

The lightning bolt—that's what did it. I'm in a hospital somewhere and I'm having a dream that I'm in the battle of Gettysburg. I'm going to wake up and everything will be okay.

The man rose to his feet and began rolling up his blanket. He was short, with a beard and a worn grey uniform. Randy got up and stuffed his blanket into his pack.

"Look, Wes, or whoever you are, I am going to say it again and I don't care if you think I'm trying to get out of something here. I am not Jed Culpepper, I am Randy Culpepper and I am having a very bad dream."

Wes just shook his head.

Just then another shell landed close by. The explosion shook the house and dust and debris rained down on the two men. Randy put his head in his hands.

If this is a dream, it's the most real dream I've ever been in. I've got to wake up!

Outside they could hear men shouting orders. Wesley took Randy by the jacket and jerked him close.

"I'm gonna tell you something! I don't care who you are, we are going back up the hill and you are going with us. So pull yourself together."

Wes gave Randy a shake and then he let go and started to head up the cellar steps. Halfway up he turned around. In his hand he held a leather pouch.

"I'm thinkin' I should leave this here. I nearly got blown to bits yesterday and if I had, there wouldn't be a letter to deliver to Ginnie."

A cold chill crept over Randy.

Ginnie's letter! The woman at the museum talked about a letter but... She was just an actress, wasn't she?

Wes walked over to the end of the room. He grabbed a stone in the foundation wall and wiggled it. It came loose in his hand. Behind the stone was a dark space. Wes stuck his hand in and pulled out a bottle. He laughed, pulled the cork and took a swig.

"Still here and still good. Willie and I used to sneak bottles of wine out of Uncle Henry's storehouse and hide them here."

He held the bottle out to Randy, but Randy shook his head. "Suit yourself." He put leather pouch in the hole, put the bottle back, and then slipped the stone back in. He turned to Randy.

"Jed, I want you to remember where this is, in case anything happens to me. And I want you to swear that if you live through this battle and I don't, you will deliver this letter to Ginnie Wade."

"Wes, this is crazy. Ginnie Wade died 150 years ago…"

Wesley stepped in front of Randy and stared into his eyes.

"Jed, I want you to swear you'll deliver this letter. Swear it!"

Randy felt an odd tightening in his stomach.

"Why is this letter so important? Who is it from?"

Wes gave Randy an odd look.

"It's from Jack, Jack Skelly. But you know that."

Jack's letter! She was waiting for Jack's letter!

"Swear it, Jed!"

Randy began to shake all over.

"All right, Wes," he whispered. "All right. I'll deliver the letter."

Wes let Randy go. He grabbed his pack and beckoned Randy to follow him. The two men went up the cellar stairs and through the door. Outside the men of the 2nd Virginia were gathering. A man in a colonel's uniform was speaking to the troops.

"Boys, the Yankees are dug in up on that hill. General Lee is going to stage an attack soon, probably on the left or center of the Union line. We've got to keep the Bluebellies occupied here to make it easier for Longstreet's men. Now yesterday we came real close to taking that hill. Steuart's boys got into the trenches on the left flank and almost broke through. That's the weak point.

Steuart will go again on the left. 2nd Virginia will go up the hill on the right, all the way to the top, and this time we have to break that line."

One of the men spoke up.

"But, Colonel, the yanks have built a real strong defense on top of that hill."

"I know, boys, I know. It will be a tough go up there. But Lee is going to mount a big attack, and Meade and Hancock will pull their troops out of the flanks to meet it if we are not holding them here."

Randy stood and listened. He knew this was a fool's game, because he knew how this battle turned out. He wanted to shout at them and tell them not to go up there, that they were only going to get slaughtered, but he looked around at the grim faces and kept his mouth shut.

I can't change history.

THE DIARY OF GINNIE WADE

Morning, July 3, 1863

We are out of bread for the soldiers so Mother and I will make some more. I must try to be brave, for that is what Jack would want me to do. Bullets have hit the house several times already this morning. The Union boys all say that Lee will attack somewhere along their line today. When will it end? I am still waiting for Jack's letter. The way things are going I will probably wait for a long time. Oh, Jack, will we ever meet again?

Ginnie stood at the kitchen counter, kneading the dough for the bread. Suddenly something hit the back door and shook the house. Ginnie started to turn when she felt a blow to her back. She lifted her arm and saw the blood pouring down. She took a step toward the front room but a terrible weakness swept over her and she cried out.

"Jack, Jack!"

Then Ginnie was falling down, down, down...

15

THE LETTER — JULY 3 – 10:00 A.M

Around ten o'clock Ewell's Corp began the attack. They formed in ranks and began to move toward the hill. Wes whispered to Randy.

"Stay close. I know every rock on this hill and every bit of cover. Willie and David and I used to play war up here all the time. And keep your head down. Whether you want to believe it or not, those are real bullets up there."

He smiled at his own joke, but Randy didn't think it was funny.

I've got to wake up; I've got to get out of here!

The troops moved forward. They came to the creek they had crossed in their retreat the night before and splashed across. The trees and brush were thick along the bank. The air was heavy and oppressive. Off to the left they could see more troops moving around the bottom of the hill. Wes smiled at some memory.

"This is Rock Creek, Jed. We used to play here on long summer days, catching crawfish and fishing for Bluegill. That was a long time ago."

A shell came in and exploded on the hillside in front of them.

"Them dang Yankees have batteries up on top. This is going to be hard going."

Randy looked at the stern faces of the men around him.

I can't go up there. We're all going to get killed.

Randy hesitated and Wesley saw it.

"Don't be thinkin' about runnin' away. I'll shoot you myself if you do."

They came to the bottom of the hill and started up. More shells started coming in. Men began to go down. The horrifying whistle of canister shot flickered between the trees and here and there big holes began to be cut in the line. The snap of musket fire began to sound all along the line.

A man in a sergeant's uniform came alongside.

"Keep your line, boys!" he shouted. "On, you Virginians!"

Randy could see the Union defenses up above. He knew how strong they were.

"Wes," he whispered, "we can't take that hill. I'm telling you that the I Corps and the XI Corps moved in there last night and reinforced Greene. He's got enough men to keep up a constant fire. He'll rotate men in and out of those trenches to reload and we're going to walk right into it. We don't stand a chance."

Wes gave Randy a strange look.

"Now how do you know that? You was with me all night."

Randy grabbed Wesley's arm and swung him around. Shells were whistling overhead. Musket balls cut the leaves of the trees. The air was filled with smoke and the screams of wounded men. He began to shout at Wesley.

"I'm telling you, Wes, I am not Jed Culpepper. I am Randy Culpepper, Jed's great-great grandson, and I know everything about this battle, every last detail! At one o'clock, Lee is going to send Pickett and twelve thousand men straight at the center of the Union line. They're going to get annihilated. Pickett is going to lose sixty percent of his men. He's going to march across a mile of open ground in a line one mile long. He's going to meet cannon fire from every point on that hill—from Cemetery Ridge to Little Round Top. He will be cut to pieces before he gets to the Emmetsburg Road. Lewis Armistead will get over the wall at the angle with a few hundred men, but he'll be killed and his men captured. On July 4, the Army of Northern Virginia will march out of this town with its tail between its legs. In two years Lee will surrender at Appomattox Courthouse."

Wes grabbed Randy's hand and forced him to let go. He stared at Randy. The outburst had struck home. For the first time Wesley Culp had an uncertain look on his face.

"You can't possibly know that."

"Wes, I'll tell you what else I know. We're going to be finished with this attack by eleven o'clock. We're not going to come close to breaking their line. Instead, the Yankees will sweep us off this hill and… and you're going to be dead."

Wesley looked straight ahead and then he shrugged his shoulders.

"If I die, I die. Everybody dies sometime."

The fire from up the hill began to pour down on them in an unceasing hail of death. Shells burst around them. Up ahead they saw the big tree where they had fought the night before. Randy and Wes scrambled behind the tree and looked out. There was chaos all around them. The man in the colonel's uniform shouted at his men.

"Keep going, boys! Don't stop now!"

Wes looked at Randy and smiled a sad smile.

"Come on, friend."

Then he stepped out from behind the tree.

Ssssssst whump!

Something hit Wes a powerful blow and spun him around. Randy watched in terror as Wes went down in a heap, right at the foot of the big tree. Randy crawled out from behind the trunk, grabbed Wes' arm and pulled him back. When he let go his hand came away wet and sticky. He knew it was blood—real blood.

Wes coughed and Randy saw blood come out of his mouth. He struggled to speak.

"I'm shot good, Jed. Right through the lung, I think..."

Wes coughed up more blood.

"...Pretty sure I'm finished. You must tell my sisters."

Randy knelt beside Wes. Wes looked up at Randy. Randy could barely hear him.

"We been in a lot of tough fights, Jed, and we've helped each other out. Now you have to get your head clear and do one more thing for me. Find my sisters in town. Show them where I am. Tell them to come get me."

Wesley took his arm and pulled him close. Randy put his ear close to Wesley's mouth.

"Go get my sisters, Jed. Tell them to come to the big tree, that's where I am."

"But, Wes...where are your sisters?"

"Jed, please, I'm dyin'. My sisters, Anna and Julia – they live right in town. Go get them, Jed. Bring them here."

Wes rose up on his arm. A horrible strength animated his face.

"Go get them, now! And then go get the letter. I swore to Jack that I would make sure his letter gets delivered. You've got to do it, Jed. I'm done for."

He fell back and Randy watched the light fade from his eyes. Blood gushed from the corner of Wes' mouth. More bullets whizzed by. Randy could hear the snap of tree limbs being cut by cannon balls. He could hear the whine of mine´ balls spanging off rocks. All around him the men who were still on their feet were turning and running back down the hill. Suddenly absolute horror gripped him. He grabbed his rifle, stood up and ran as fast as he could down the hill toward Gettysburg. Bullets whistled all around him. He was almost down the hill when two shells bracketed him. The twin explosions blew him off his feet and into the air. He felt a blow on his left side like a mule kick. He landed awkwardly about five feet down the hill. Randy lay there, gasping. Dirt and leaves filled his mouth. Hands pulled him up and began to drag him along until he found his feet. He kept running.

Check for blood!

His left hand began to hurt terribly. He looked down and saw blood streaming from his hand and his arm. His musket was dented right where he held it. He stopped behind a big rock and looked at his hand. It was mangled and he could see the bones where his skin had been shredded. He saw that there was a hole torn in his pants and blood ran down his leg. He felt weak and his ears were still ringing. Men ran past the rock. He saw a man sprint by and then a shell hit him and the man was gone, leaving nothing but a bloody spray on the rock. Randy felt his own blood run down his leg and his arm.

Got to help Wes, got to get the letter...

Randy took two more stumbling steps and the lights went out.

16

GOING BACK — JULY 3 – 12:00 P.M

Randy Culpepper opened his eyes. He lay on a rough table in the red barn at the bottom of Culp's Hill. The top of the table was slippery with blood. A Confederate doctor stood a few feet away, wiping off a sharp knife. Randy felt a sharp pain in his hand. He looked down and saw that his hand was wrapped in a bandage.

"My hand! What happened to my hand?"

The doctor smiled at him.

"You're one of the lucky ones, son. A couple of men grabbed you and dragged you down off that bloody hill in time to keep you from bleeding to death. You only lost two fingers. Your rifle saved your life. Something hit the stock where you were holding it and glanced off. Your leg was gashed in passing but it's bandaged up and you'll walk out of here. The hand's going to hurt for a while and you have to keep it clean so it doesn't get infected, but you should be going home for a long rest."

Randy struggled to sit up. He wanted to get off the bloody table. The doctor saw his discomfort and smiled.

"Don't worry, son, that's not all your blood. There's been a lot worse happen on that table today."

He turned back to his instruments. Randy slipped off the table and stood unsteadily.

"Where's my musket, Doctor?"

The doctor pointed at the door of the tent. There were ten or twenty muskets stacked there.

"Take your pick. Most of the boys who owned those won't be needing them."

Randy saw his Enfield among the muskets. It had a large dent in the stock.

But it already had that dent...or did it?

As he limped out of the tent he saw the man in the sergeant's uniform.

"Culpepper, what are you doin' here?"

Randy held up his bandaged hand.

"Lost two of my fingers, Sergeant!"

I'm going to wake up...I've got to wake up...before I get killed!

"Where's Culp?"

"He's...he's up on the hill, by the big tree. He was shot really bad. I think he's dead. I'm supposed to find his sisters but I don't know where..."

The sergeant pointed back down the street toward town.

"Julia and Anna? They live just down there. Big house on the left with the rose bushes by the porch."

Randy limped down the street and turned into the gate. He made his way up on the porch and knocked. A pretty woman opened the door and looked out. Randy spoke through the pain.

"Are you Julia?"

"No, I'm Anna, who are you?"

"I'm Wesley's friend."

"Oh, you must be Jed Culpepper."

Anna looked at Randy's hand and a look of fear came over her face.

"Where...where is Wesley?"

"He's up by the big tree. He's been shot. I think he's dying. He sent me to get you."

Anna's eyes opened wide. She turned and shouted into the house.

"Julia, get your shawl! Wesley's hurt and we must go to him."

Randy took a step toward Anna.

"There's one more thing. I promised Wes I would deliver a letter...to Ginnie Wade."

Anna looked at him strangely.

"The letter doesn't matter anymore, Jed. A Confederate sharpshooter shot Ginnie Wade this morning as she was baking bread for the Union troops. She's dead."

I knew that!

Suddenly to the north of town a huge rumbling roar began to shake the earth. The two women put their hands over their ears. Randy looked toward Cemetery Hill. It was blanketed with smoke. He took two steps toward the street. He knew what was happening. He could hear his Grandfather's bitter voice, telling the story...

That's Alexander's artillery pouring everything they have into the center of the Union line. He'll shoot too high and miss most of his targets. In a little while Longstreet will send George Pickett and his division up that hill into death and glory. They'll march in beautiful formations, a mile of men with their drums beating, and the flags of Virginia waving. Hancock will be waiting at the top of the long rise. Before they are even halfway across the open ground, the Rebel line will be enfiladed with cannon fire and muskets. They'll be cut to ribbons. A few of the bravest will get over the stone wall, but they will be shot and captured. Pickett will lose all of his commanders and most of his men. When the smoke clears, the Union troops will still hold the high ground. Lee will withdraw from the North tomorrow... and the Civil War will be over...

Randy turned back to Julia and Anna. They were holding

each other and screaming. The earth was shaking with the thunderous explosions and the ground rocked. Randy's head began to swim. The light began to dim and then he fainted...

17

BACK TO GETTYSBURG — JULY 4, 2013

A strange whirring sound, cool air, smooth sheets, a slow beeping...

Randy's eyes snapped open. He gasped, lifted himself up, and looked around. The whirring sound was an electric fan on a table by the bed. The beeping was coming from a machine behind him. He was lying in a clean bed in a small room in...

I'm in a hospital! I'm back! Oh, thank you, God!

He fell back on the pillow. Just then the door opened and a nurse in a white uniform walked in.

"Good morning, Mr. Culpepper. How are you? How's the hand this morning?"

The hand? Why the hand?

Randy looked down. His arm was completely bandaged from the tips of the fingers to the elbow, but he didn't feel any pain, only a dull ache.

"What happened to my hand, nurse?"

"I should probably get the doctor," she said. She turned and left.

What happened to my hand?

In a few minutes the nurse returned with a young man. He smiled at Randy and came to the side of the bed.

"Well, good morning, Mr. Culpepper. I'm Doctor Rosenthal. And how are we this morning?"

"Doctor, what happened to my hand?"

"You were struck by lightning, Mr. Culpepper. The bolt traveled through your body and exited through your left hand, where you were holding your musket."

"But my hand...?"

"The bolt didn't kill you when it hit, but it did a lot of damage on the way out. Your fourth and fifth fingers were shredded. I'm sorry to tell you this, but we had to amputate them. There was hardly anything left and we couldn't save them."

"What! You amputated my fingers?"

"Yes, sir. I'm sorry, but it was the only course of action we could take."

Randy fell back on the pillow.

Wait. My fingers were shot off... in the battle. But that couldn't be. It was only a dream.

The doctor saw the look on Randy's face and spoke.

"You won't lose the use of your hand, and otherwise you seem to be all right, except for the gash on your leg."

"My leg?"

"Yes, when you were knocked unconscious, you fell against something and gashed your leg pretty badly. I had to take a few stitches."

Outside there were explosions. Randy jumped.

"What's that?"

"The big re-enactment has started, Mr. Culpepper. It's the 150th anniversary of the Battle of Gettysburg. This will be going on for three days."

"What day is it?"

"July 4, 2013, Mr. Culpepper."

"But the battle was over yesterday. We couldn't take that bloody hill."

Randy could see the doctor gave the nurse a look.

"You must be thinking about the re-enactment put on by the other group. That ended on Friday."

"No, I'm telling you I was in a battle yesterday. That's how I lost my fingers."

"Mr. Culpepper, there was no battle yesterday. You were hit by lightning two days ago and you've been unconscious and under heavy sedation. You are going to have some residual effects—particularly with your memory. Now I would recommend that you get some more rest. I'll look in on you later."

The doctor turned and left the room, followed by the nurse. Randy stared blankly at the wall.

So it was just a dream, after all...

SPECIAL DELIVERY — JULY 5

Randy walked unsteadily out the front door of the hospital. He didn't have too much pain, but his leg was stiff and he was sore all over his body. Outside the streets were filled with men and women in Civil War era costumes. There was a country band playing on a stage just down the street and overhead fireworks filled the night sky.

Where did I leave my car? Hope I don't have a ticket...Baltimore Street...it's on Baltimore. Turn right on South Street, walk three blocks, turn right.

More fireworks blasts filled the sky. The explosions made Randy jump.

Easy, Randy! You're back...it was all a nightmare!

The night was hot and humid. Randy felt the charge in the air that precedes a thunderstorm. He was still dressed in his uniform as he turned on Baltimore and walked slowly toward his SUV. Up ahead he saw the sign: *Jennie Wade House – Museum – Ghostly Images – Tours*. Another flash filled the sky, followed by a deep rumble. Randy ducked under a tree in front of the Museum. The bright light died away

That was lightning!

And then, he saw it again—the strange glowing light coalescing around a figure at the top of the stairs. And... the young woman was there—Ginnie Wade! The deep cold swept over Randy. She came a step closer and held out her hand.

"Did you bring it?"

"Bring it?"

"The letter, Jack's letter. I can't ever leave until I have the letter. Please..."

There was another flash of lightning that was so bright it blinded Randy for a moment. When he could see, the woman was gone from the steps... In the window, a single candle flickering, the woman standing behind the glass, staring, waiting...waiting...

Randy felt the shaking begin. He was freezing...

So it did happen after all. Somehow I am part of a strange vignette—the sad tale of two lovers and the letter that never came. She's been waiting all these years...

Then he remembered.

The letter! I know where the letter is. I was there when Wesley hid it!

Then at last it all came clear and Randy knew why he had been brought back to Gettysburg. He turned and walked back up Baltimore Street as fast as he could. When he got to Middle Street, he turned right. His leg was aching and his hand hurt, but he kept walking. The streets were jammed with people—he passed the bandstand where the country group was playing. The explosions from the fireworks mixed with occasional flashes of lightning—the people cheering—the music...

There! The farmhouse! Behind the house was the barn where they had amputated his fingers. There was the hill where Wesley died. Randy looked around. The sign on the farmhouse door said *Closed.* Randy walked around to the back and went to the cellar door. There was a padlock on it. He started to turn away.

Pull on it!

Randy looked around to see who had spoken—no one was there! He reached out his good hand, took hold of the lock and pulled. It opened with a click. Randy looked at it in surprise. He opened the door. The cellar stairs were dark, but there was a switch on the wall at the top of the stairs and he clicked it on. Down at the bottom was a single bulb on the wall. The cellar smelled old, musty, damp. He eased down the stairs, favoring his leg.

He put it in the wall—over there.

Randy moved to the back wall. He began to push and pull on the stones—no, no, no, yes! A stone moved under his hand. He wiggled it back and forth and it moved forward in its hole. He pulled on it and then it slid right out. He reached in and felt something smooth and cold—glass! He pulled out an old green wine bottle, corked and half-filled with a dark liquid.

Wes and Willie's wine stash!

Randy smiled. Then he reached back into the hole. There! He felt the texture of leather under his fingers. He pulled it out and stared at the black pouch. Slowly he opened it. Inside were some scraps of paper and an envelope. He took out the envelope and examined it in the dim light. There was a dark smear on the corner…

Blood!

Written in an unsteady hand across the envelope were two words: *Ginnie Wade.* The letter!

So it is true! Jack Skelly gave a letter to Wesley Culp to take to Ginnie! And here it is!

The envelope was not sealed. He held it against his chest with his bandaged hand and opened it with the other. There were two items: A folded piece of paper and a picture. The picture was of a young man in a formal suit with a white shirt and a bow tie. He had blond hair and a serious expression. He was handsome. He unfolded the paper and read.

My Dearest Ginnie,

I am sorry that I haven't written sooner, but we have had a hard time of it here in Virginia. I started this letter several times but I only finished it today at Winchester. To my shame, I must tell you that the Rebs beat us pretty soundly, and I have a bad wound. I am hoping to somehow post this letter so you will know of my condition and not live in uncertainty.

I am writing this because I fear we may not see each other again, soon. I am going to a Reb hospital and if I survive, they will send me to Libby prison. I don't want to frighten you, but the truth is, my fate is quite uncertain. So, I need to ask you something that has been on my heart for a long time, so you will know truly how I feel about you. I don't know how long I will be away. It may be for years, but when I do come home, I want you to become my wife. I have loved you since we were children and I want to spend the rest of my life with you. It is my earnest hope that you will reciprocate my feelings and say yes.

When this war is over I am hoping to see you again—when the hills of Pennsylvania are ablaze with color and we can walk together again on a bright fall morning, as we did so often when we were young. Wait for me, Ginnie. Wait for me. I will see you again, someday.

I love you with all my heart

Jack

RANDY FOLDED the letter and put it back into the envelope. He walked slowly up the cellar stairs. Outside, he looked up at the sky. Thunderclouds were still rolling through, but behind them the sky was clearing. The fireworks lit the clouds with flashes of color. Randy slowly made his way back to Baltimore Street and limped toward the museum. His leg ached but his task was almost done. As he came to the steps, he looked up and she was standing there, shimmering in the shadows. Randy slowly walked up the steps. She held out a trembling hand. Randy handed her the envelope.

"I'm sorry, I read it without thinking."

He could see what seemed to be a blush steal across her pale face. She took out the picture and gazed at it for a long time. Then she opened the letter with trembling hands. She read silently and then pressed the message to her breast and bowed her head.

"You did love me, Jack," she said quietly.

Behind him, Randy heard steps coming up the walk. He turned to look. A young man dressed in a Union uniform stood at the bottom of the stairs. He looked older than the picture in the letter and he had grown a mustache. One sleeve of his uniform was pinned up. He held out his hand.

"Come, Ginnie," he said. "Now we can go."

Ginnie slipped the letter into her pocket and walked down the stairs. At the bottom she hesitated. The young man reached out and took her hand and pulled her to him. They stood looking at each other for a long time. She turned her face up to his and he kissed her gently. Her arms went around him and she held him for a long time. She whispered ,"Jack, my Jack." And then, hand-in-hand, they turned and walked away. Randy watched them go. At the gate, they paused and Ginnie looked back.

"Thank you," she said softly.

Together they walked up Baltimore Street. Randy watched until he could not see them anymore. He turned to go. And then he saw a man in a gray uniform standing in the shadow of the trees across the street. Randy could just make him out. He was short, with a full beard. He, too, was watching as the couple walked away. Randy could just barely see his face. The man smiled a sad smile and then he turned and started to walk away into the shadows.

"Goodbye, Wes."

The man turned. He looked at Randy and lifted his hand in a salute.

"Goodbye...friend!"

And then the man simply faded away.

ABOVE RANDY the skies of Gettysburg cleared and one by one the stars came out. Low on the horizon he saw a shooting star...then another...and another. A furious last burst of fireworks filled the night sky with color and flame. The explosions echoed from the long ridges where the most terrible battle in American history had been fought. Randy sighed, walked down the steps, and limped toward the old SUV. As he walked he knew that tonight, for the first time in a long time, there was peace in Gettysburg.

EPILOGUE

Of the many legends and stories that surround the great battle at Gettysburg, perhaps none is so heart wrenching as that of Ginnie Wade, Jack Skelly and Wesley Culp. It is a story that, like most folk tales, has grown more fanciful through the years. I, being the hopeless romantic that I am, have tried to bring the loose ends together in proposing at least a happy ending to the tale. Concerning the main characters, I have added a few footnotes here to give clarity to the final disposition of their lives.

WESLEY CULP: *After the battle, Wesley Culp's sisters went up to the hill where they had all played as children and searched the hillside for his body. There are several versions of what happened. Some say that he had been hastily buried under the tree where he died. Julia and Anna searched under many trees but all they ever found was the stock of his musket with his initials carved into it. Another story says that the sisters found him and, with the help of some soldiers, carried his body to his Uncle Henry's farm where they buried Wes Culp in the basement. Other citizens of Gettysburg claimed that his sisters took his body by night, so as not to offend his neighbors who considered Wesley a* traitor, and buried it secretly in Evergreen Cemetery on Cemetery Ridge. Wesley's brother, William, and cousin, David, survived the war. From the day of the battle until he died, William never allowed Wesley's name to be spoken in his presence.

GINNIE WADE: Ginnie Wade was the only civilian killed in the Battle of Gettysburg. On the morning of July 3, she woke up early and began baking bread for the Union soldiers. The legend goes that a Confederate sharpshooter, thinking that the houses between his position and the Union picket line at the base of Cemetery ridge had been vacated, fired a few practice rounds at the back door of Georgia McClellan's home. One of those shots passed through the outside kitchen door, went through the door between the kitchen and the parlor, and struck Ginnie Wade in the back left shoulder blade piercing her heart and killing her instantly. The holes where the bullet passed through can be seen to this day. Union soldiers, alerted by her mother's screams, ran to the house and, seeing Ginnie's lifeless body, carried it to the basement where it remained all that day. The next day, she was buried in the garden at Georgia's house. Nearly two years later, she was moved to Evergreen Cemetery and is there to this day.

JACK SKELLY: Jack never came back to Gettysburg, at least not in this life. Jack died from his wound on July 15, 1863, just twelve days after the Battle of Gettysburg. He was originally buried in Winchester, Virginia, in the Lutheran Cemetery. A little over a year after his death, Jack's brother, Daniel, moved Jack's body to the Evergreen Cemetery in Gettysburg. He now rests just seventy-seven yards southwest of his beloved Ginnie.

THE LETTER: No one ever found the letter that Jack Skelly sent to Ginnie by the hand of Wesley Culp, so we will never really know what *it contained. This story only offers possibilities so the true contents of the letter will forever remain a mystery. All we know for sure is that Ginnie and Jack, and perhaps Wesley, though not joined in life, rest together in the beautiful cemetery on top of the ridge looking down on the Pennsylvania countryside that was the scene of the greatest battle ever fought on American soil.*

ABOUT THE AUTHOR

Patrick E. Craig is a lifelong writer and musician. After retiring from the ministry in 2007 he concentrated on writing and publishing fiction books. He has published six Amish novels, two YA mystery books, one World War II historical novel, two Anthologies of Amish stories, a creative non-fiction memoir and this book. He lives in Idaho with his wife Judy.

ALSO BY PATRICK E. CRAIG

A Quilt For Jenna

The Road Home

Jenny's Choice

The Amish Heiress

The Amish Princess

The Mennonite Queen

The Mystery of Ghost Dancer Ranch

The Lost Coast

The Amish Menorah and Other Stories

A Christmas Collection

Say Goodbye To The River

Far On The Ringing Plains w/Murray Pura

The Scepter and The Isle w/Murray Pura

Contact Patrick at pec@patrickecraig.com

Website: https://www.patrickecraig.com